THE MOUSE FAMILY ROBINSON

DICK KING-SMITH

THE MOUSE FAMILY ROBINSON

ILLUSTRATED BY
NICK BRUEL

Roaring Brook Press
New York

First published in Great Britain by Puffin Books, an imprint of the Penguin Group
Published in the United States by Roaring Brook Press,
a division of Holtzbrinck Publishing Holdings Limited Partnership
175 Fifth Avenue, New York, New York 10010

Library of Congress Cataloging-in-Publication Data
King-Smith, Dick.
The mouse family Robinson / Dick King-Smith ; illustrated by Nick Bruel.
— 1st American ed.
p. cm.
Summary: After a close call with the cat who stalks the hallways, a family of wild mice, including
adventurous, young Beaumont and elderly Uncle Brown, emigrates to a more mouse-friendly
house down the block.
ISBN-13: 978-1-59643-326-7
ISBN-10: 1-59643-326-4
[1. Mice--Fiction. 2. Family life--Fiction.] I. Bruel, Nick, ill. II. Title.
PZ7.K5893Mq 2008
[Fic]--dc22
2008011139

Roaring Brook Press books are available for special promotions and premiums.
For details contact: Director of Special Markets, Holtzbrinck Publishers.

Book design by Jaime Putorti

First Roaring Brook Press Edition August 2008
Printed in the United States of America
1 3 5 7 9 10 8 6 4 2

FOR LOUISE AND THE FAMILY GENEREAUX

—N.B.

John Robinson and Mr. Brown were next-door neighbors. That is to say, they both lived under the kitchen floor, for John Robinson and Mr. Brown were house mice.

John was a young chap. He was respectful toward his neighbor, who was very old, and always addressed him as "Mr. Brown." Mr.

Brown, John knew, now lived alone because his wife had been eaten by the cat.

There came an evening when John's young wife, Janet, told him that he was to become a father for the first time. She was tearing up bits of newspaper to make a comfy nest.

"Gosh!" said John. "You mean you're going to have a baby?"

GOSH!

2

"Babies," said Janet.

She has gotten fat lately, come to think of it, said John to himself.

"When?" he asked.

"Very soon."

"Gosh! How many?"

"How do I know, you stupid mouse?" said Janet. "Now push off and leave me in peace."

As John was hurrying under the kitchen floor, he met his neighbor coming back home.

"Good evening, Mr. Brown," he said.

"Evening, John," said Mr. Brown. "How's life?"

"Wonderful!" replied John. "I am going to be a father."

"For the first time, eh?"

"Yes. I believe you've had a large number of children, Mr. Brown, haven't you?"

"Dozens. So many that I've gone and forgotten most of their names. My late wife and I used to rely on the alphabet."

"The alphabet?" said John.

"Yes. Start with *A*—Adam, let's say, or Alice— and keep going till you get to Z. That gives you twenty-six names."

"You mean you've had twenty-six children, Mr. Brown?"

"Seventy-eight, actually, John. We went through the alphabet three times."

"Gosh!" said John.

"Xs and Zs," said Mr. Brown, "are the hardest

ones to put names to, but we managed. Why don't you try the same trick?"

"I will, I will," said John. "Thanks, Mr. Brown, that's a good idea."

The young mouse and his elderly neighbor chatted for a while, mainly about food. A nest under the kitchen floor, as both knew well, is the best place for mice to live. Those clumsy giants called humans were always dropping bits of food on the floor, and if a mouse was bold enough, there were lovely things to eat in the pantry.

Talking about food made John feel hungry, and after a while he said, "I must be going, Mr. Brown, if you'll excuse me."

"Of course, John," Mr. Brown replied, "and I'm so pleased to hear your good news. Please give my regards to your wife."

"I will," replied John, "and thank you."

Poor old fellow, he thought, remembering what had happened to Mrs. Brown.

Now evening had turned to night, and the giants had all gone up the stairs to bed. John Robinson popped out of a mousehole and began to search the kitchen floor, all his senses alert, especially for the squeak of the cat flap.

He was in luck. Someone had spilled half a dozen cornflakes: not much for a giant, but a feast for a mouse.

His hunger satisfied, he made his way home.

Will Janet have had the babies yet? he wondered. *How many will there be? How many will be boys; how many girls?*

The answers to these questions, John found, were "yes," "six," and "three of each."

"What should we call them?" John asked.

"You can choose, if you want," said Janet.

I'll use Mr. Brown's alphabet method, thought John. *Six kids, that's A to F. Let's see now . . . I must think up some unusual names because I'm sure my children will grow up to be unusual mice.*

John Robinson spent the rest of the night

deciding what to call his newborn sons and daughters. As dawn broke, he knew he had found six perfect names. *And*, he said to himself, *I must tell Mr. Brown. I'm sure he'd like to know,* and he hurried along one of the runways beneath the kitchen floor.

"Mr. Brown," he said, when he had found his neighbor, "Janet's had six babies. I thought you'd like to know."

"Congratulations, John!" said Mr. Brown. "Got names for them?"

"I have," said John. "Ambrose, Beaumont, Camilla, Desdemona, Eustace, and Felicity. What d'you think?"

"Brilliant!" said Mr. Brown. "Three boys and

three girls, eh? It's a start. Twenty more babies and you'll have finished your first alphabet of names."

Gosh! said John to himself. To think that his neighbor had seventy-eight kids!

Even as he thought this, they heard, through the floorboards above their heads, the squeak of the cat flap.

At the sound the two mice froze, even though they were quite safe under the kitchen floor-boards. They looked at one another and Mr. Brown sighed deeply.

I know what he's thinking, said John to himself. *How dreadful if such a thing ever happened to my*

Janet. If only that horrible cat didn't live here.

"I must be getting back to my family, Mr. Brown," he said after a while.

"Of course," replied Mr. Brown. "I'd love to come and see them when they're a little older. Could I?"

"Please do," said John.

The mousekins had been born naked and blind, but later on, when they had grown coats of fur (gray, of course) and had opened their beady little eyes, John invited Mr. Brown around. Proudly he and Janet stood on either side of their six children while the old mouse looked them over.

"They're lovely!" he said. "I do congratulate you both."

"Thank you," replied Janet, and "Thank you, sir," said John.

"When they're a bit older," said Mr. Brown, "perhaps they'll come and visit me?" and, a few weeks later, one of them did.

14

Beaumont was the brightest and the most adventurous of the six mousekins, and he was the first to venture out of the nest and start to explore the spaces under the kitchen floor. Soon he came upon a mouse run that led upward and, following it, stuck his head out of a hole in the molding. He found himself staring across the kitchen floor. Beside the stove, he could see, was a basket.

Beaumont was not only bright and adventurous, but also curious. *I wonder what's in that basket?* he thought.

He was halfway across the kitchen floor when two things happened. First, he heard a voice coming from the hole he'd just left, a frantic voice that cried, "Come back! Come back! Quickly! Quickly!"

Then he saw a face—a face that rose above the rim of the basket—a fearsome furry face with yellow eyes, which were fixed upon him.

Beaumont turned and dashed back toward the hole in the molding just in time. Above him, he heard the scrabble of the cat's claws as it scratched at the mousehole. Before him, he saw an old mouse.

"Oh!" squeaked Beaumont. "Was it you who called me back?"

"It was," replied Mr. Brown. "That was a narrow squeak, young fellow. What's your name?"

"I'm Beaumont Robinson."

"One of John's children?"

"Yes. Who are you?"

"I'm Mr. Brown."

"Oh, you're Dad's friend."

"I like to think so."

"The one who came to visit us?"

"Yes."

"Have you got any children?"

"Seventy-eight," replied Mr. Brown. *Though goodness only knows how many are still alive,* he thought.

"Gosh!" said Beaumont (a word he had learned from his father). "My dad told us your wife got eaten by the cat."

"She did, Beaumont," said Mr. Brown. *And so would you have been,* he thought, *if I hadn't happened to look out just in time. Yours would have been a very short life.*

"Well," said Beaumont, "isn't there any way we can get rid of the beastly thing?"

"Alas, no," said Mr. Brown. "Cats can kill mice, but, unfortunately, mice can't kill cats."

"Oh," said Beaumont. "So we have to wait till it dies of old age, do we?"

"That might be a long time," said Mr. Brown.

"What can we do, then?"

"Nothing, I'm afraid, Beaumont. The giants have got a cat, and we have got to live with it."

Have we? thought Beaumont. *What if . . . ? No, I'd better ask Dad first.*

"Got to go," he said. "Nice talking to you, Uncle Brown."

When he got home, he said, "I've been talking to Uncle Brown, Dad."

"Have you indeed?" said John. *I bet the old chap's pleased at being called that,* he thought.

"Yes," said Beaumont. "He saved my life, Dad. I went up into the kitchen and the cat nearly got me!"

"Gosh!" said John.

"Uncle Brown says we just have to live with the beastly thing."

"Well, he's right, Beaumont. We have no choice."

"Yes, we have, Dad," said Beaumont. "If the cat won't leave us, we can leave the cat."

"What d'you mean?"

"We can move to another house, one without a cat. We can emigrate, Dad," said Beaumont.

"Emigrate?" said John to Beaumont.

"Yes, Dad."

"But . . . how will I know if another house has a cat or not?"

"If it has a cat, it'll smell of the beastly thing. If it doesn't, it won't. Simple, Dad."

"It'll take me an awfully long time to inspect every house on the street."

"It would if it was just you, Dad," said Beaumont, "but what if we all helped, eh, Mom?"

"I certainly will," said Janet, "but you kids are too small to take the risk."

"We're not," said Beaumont, turning to the other five mousekins, "are we? We can help, can't we?"

And with one voice, Ambrose and Camilla and Desdemona and Eustace and Felicity cried, "Yes!"

Janet looked proudly at her six children.

"All right," she said, "but not just yet. Wait till you've grown a lot bigger."

"And a lot faster on your feet," added John. "There'll be

other cats in other houses on the street, and dogs, too, and then there's all the traffic. Wait till you're as big as Mom and me."

"But that'll be ages, Dad!" said Beaumont.

"Do as your father says," said Janet sharply, and in unison, Ambrose and Beaumont and Camilla and Desdemona and Eustace and Felicity muttered, "Yes, Mom."

*   *   *

In fact, a month went by before John and Janet allowed the six mousekins out of the house.

John had established a route—from under the kitchen floor through a runway that led down into the cellar, and from the cellar up and out through a grating onto the sidewalk outside.

Janet made a plan of action. Their house was number 24, even-numbered like all those on that side of the street. Each night she and the three girls would work their way down the road, somehow making their way into number 22, then number 20, and so on, while John and the three boys would be inspecting each house up the street—numbers 26, 28, 30, and so on.

"Let's just hope they don't all have cats in them, Janet," said John. "I don't fancy having to cross the road."

But luck was on their side.

On the fourth night, Janet and the girls explored number 16 and came home excited and delighted to report that there was no smell or sign of cat or dog in that house.

"All we could smell," said Janet, "was mice!"

"Great!" said John. "We'll emigrate there."

Five of the mousekins squeaked with joy, but Beaumont said, "What about Uncle Brown?"

"What about him?" said the others.

"He'll be lonely without us."

"Beaumont's right," said Janet. "He might like to come too, don't you think, John? Why don't you ask him?"

Of course we must, thought John. *He saved Beaumont's life.*

So one of the girls—Felicity, it was—was sent to fetch Mr. Brown.

"We're moving, Mr. Brown," said John when

the old mouse arrived. "To get away from the cat."

Just what I was thinking, said Mr. Brown to himself.

"We're going to number 16; there's no cat there," said John.

"We wondered if you'd like to come with us," said Janet.

"It's very kind of you, Mrs. Robinson—"

"'Janet,' please," she interrupted.

"—very kind of you, er, Janet, as I was saying, but I'm sure you'd rather be on your own as a family. I'll miss you, of course."

"No, you won't, Mr. Brown," said John in a masterful voice. "I insist that you come with us. Please do."

"We can't go without you, Uncle Brown," said Beaumont quietly.

Uncle, thought the old mouse. *How nice. Some of my seventy-eight children must, I hope, be alive and well, but I never see any of them. They've all gone off somewhere, so why don't I run off too?*

"Please come, Uncle Brown!" squeaked the other mousekins.

"Pleeeease!"

And then they heard the sound of the cat flap

as the cat, attracted by all the noise, came into the kitchen.

Mr. Brown looked at Janet and John and at Beaumont and the five other youngsters.

"Thank you," he said. "I'd love to."

4

Number 16 Simple Street did indeed smell quite strongly of mice, and the family who lived there wouldn't have dreamed of having a cat.

There were three giants (as mice thought of them): Mr. Black, Mrs. Black, and their son, a boy called Bill.

Bill Black had always been keen on pet animals, especially mice, and, once he was old enough, his parents let him keep some. These were pet mice, fancy mice, of course, not ordinary house mice like the Robinsons and Mr. Brown.

Bill had mice of several different colors: he had white ones with pink eyes and white ones with black eyes and chocolate ones and fawn ones and plum-colored ones and mice with special black markings called Dutch.

By the time Bill was ten years old, he had so many pet mice that his father and mother let him use a little spare room (which he called the Mousery) to keep all his different-colored mice in their neat cages. By the time that Janet Robinson and her daughters had come into number 16 to have a sniff around, there were thirty pet mice in the Mousery, not counting babies, so that the smell of them was pretty strong.

No matter, thought Janet. *There's not the faintest smell of cat.*

At the next full moon, all the migrants made their move down the street from number 24.

John Robinson—after politely asking the advice of old Mr. Brown—had

 decided that though traveling in bright moonlight might be

 risky, it would alert them to any cats or other dangers on the way, and at midnight the emigration began.

John led the file of mice: behind him came Beaumont and Eustace and Ambrose. Next came Mr. Brown, followed by Felicity and Desdemona and Camilla, while Janet brought up the rear.

After they'd gone a little way, Beaumont said to his father, "I'm just going to drop back to make sure Uncle B's all right."

It was just as well he did, for at that very

moment, a dog barked loudly from inside number 22, and Mr. Brown, frightened by the sudden noise, slipped off the sidewalk. He seemed to be about to cross the road.

"Come back! Come back! Quickly! Quickly!" cried Beaumont, and the old mouse obeyed just in time, for a car came roaring down the road, only just missing Mr. Brown.

"Oh, thank you, Beaumont, my boy!" Mr. Brown panted as he scrambled back over the curb. *Another narrow squeak*, he thought. *I save him from the cat; he saves me from the car.*

After that, they passed numbers 20 and 18—cat smells coming from both of these houses—and mercifully arrived safely at number 16 and made

their way in. The scent of mice was everywhere, but the nine travelers from number 24 soon found the room where it was strongest: the Mousery.

The cages in which Bill Black kept his fancy mice stood on top of two long, low tables. John Robinson shinnied up the leg of one of them and found himself in front of the first cage, staring into the red eyes of a mouse that was otherwise pure white. It was a buck, John could tell from its scent, and a bad-tempered buck at that. Coming

close to the bars of its cage it said in a sneery voice, "Get lost. We don't want common house mice in here. These cages are for well-bred fancy mice only, so sling your hook, ugly mug."

"Don't talk to me like that!" said John angrily. "Come on outside and we'll see who's the better mouse."

"Calm down, John," said Mr. Brown from the floor below. "He can't come out anyway, he's in a cage."

"Just as well for him," said John.

"Yes, but just as well for us, too," said Mr. Brown.

He turned to Janet.

"You've been very clever in your choice of house," he said. "One of the giants here keeps mice as pets, it would appear, so the place must to be free of cats. Well done, my dear Janet."

"Thank you, Mr. Brown," Janet replied. *I can't call him by his first name,* she thought, *because I don't know what it is, and I don't really want to ask him. Perhaps we'll never know what it is.*

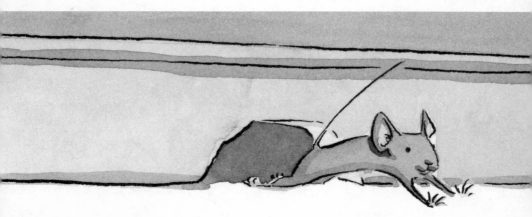

"There's lots of food around, too," she said.

"Which means," said John, "that there'll be lots of other house mice around," and at that very moment, a mouse came out through a hole in the molding.

"You're right, mate," he said to John, "but there's plenty for all of us. The giants here are lovely people, especially the smallest one of the three. No cats—as you can smell—no dogs, no traps, no poison, and they leave food all over the place. You've struck lucky, you lot. Welcome to Liberty Hall!"

"He seemed a happy sort of chap," said John to Janet as the mouse disappeared down its hole. "Don't you think so, Mr. Brown?"

"I think," said Mr. Brown, "that he and his fellows have plenty to be happy about. He's right—we have struck lucky."

For the rest of that night, they all explored the

Mousery. None of the fancy mice were as rude as the first pink-eyed white buck had been, but all were a bit standoffish.

"Shouldn't we get moving?" asked Janet as the first light of dawn came in through the window. "We don't want one of the giants to come and find us in here."

"Why not, Mom?" asked Beaumont.

"Because they might not want nine more mice in their house," said Janet. "Let's all go down that hole in the molding and find where it leads."

So they all did. As they made their way down, their sharp ears heard a lot of mouse noises. There were runways through which came sounds of mice, above and below them. They came at last to the cellar of number 16, in which there were a good many mice, all of whom greeted the newcomers in a friendly fashion.

Above their heads, Bill Black came into the Mousery in his pajamas (his bedroom was next door) to give his pets their breakfast. He filled the food dish in each cage with canary seed, made sure that all the mice had clean water to drink, and, of course, talked to the occupants of every cage. Bill was sure that pets like dogs and cats enjoyed being talked to, so why should mice be any different?

In the last cage was a

chocolate doe, all by herself because she was soon to have babies. Bill took a very small bit of broken cookie from a tin and put it down in front of her nose.

"D'you know," he said  to her, "what I'd love to do? I'd love to tame a wild mouse. I bet noone's ever done that. I'd have to catch one first though—a young one." Even as he said these last words, Bill heard a little scratching noise, and there, coming out of the hole in the molding, was a young house mouse.

Beaumont, the brightest, most adventurous, and now indeed the boldest of John and Janet's six children, had heard the sound of Bill's voice from the cellar below and had scuttled back up the runway to see what a giant looked like. Never in his short life had he seen one before.

How strange! thought Bill. *Just the kind of mouse that I need, but how do I catch it?*

Very slowly, he took another piece of cookie

from the tin. Very slowly, he moved toward the young mouse, who crouched by the hole below, whiskers twitching. Very slowly, Bill Black offered the piece of cookie to Beaumont Robinson.

They looked into each other's eyes and each had much the same feelings. They liked the look of one another.

This is a very bold little house mouse, thought Bill. *Could I make a pet of him?*

This is a very nice giant, thought Beaumont. *I'm not afraid of him at all.*

He took a bite of cookie.

"Delicious!" he said.

All Bill heard, of course, was a squeak, but it sounded like a happy squeak. Suddenly, the young mouse turned and disappeared down the hole.

"Dad!" cried Beaumont as he reached the cellar. "There's ever such a nice giant up above us. He gave me a lovely piece of cookie. Come up and see him!" and he turned and dashed up the runway again, followed by Ambrose and Camilla and Desdemona and Eustace and Felicity.

After them went Janet, calling, "Come back, children!" and after her went John, calling, "Come back, Janet!"

To his surprise, Bill found himself looking at five more mousekins, and then to his astonishment, two adult mice emerged from the hole.

Mom and Dad and six kids, he thought, and crumbled more cookie on the floor. They were all

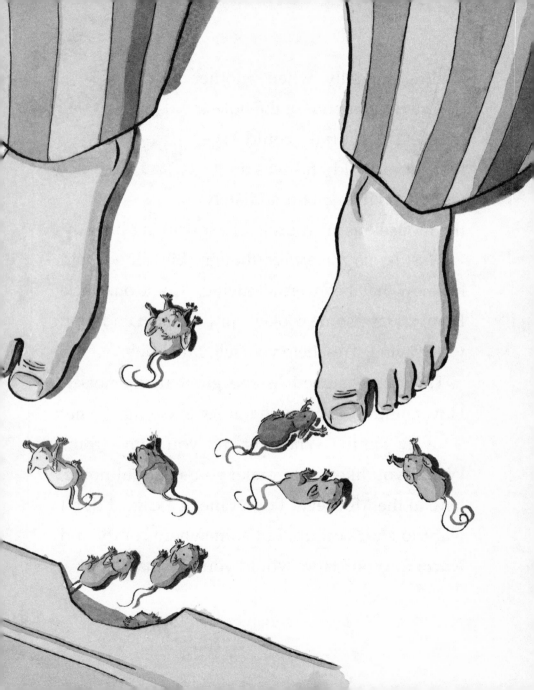

feeding greedily when another mouse came up out of the hole, a mouse that, Bill could see, looked very old and was a bit wobbly on its legs. Immediately  the mousekins surrounded it, squeaking happily.

Must be the grandfather, thought Bill. How could he know that they were all saying, "Come on, Uncle Brown! Have some cookie!" or that Janet and John were saying, "Yes, help yourself, Mr. Brown"?

The mice listened as the giant made noises. How could they know that he was saying, "What a lovely family! Wherever did you come from? Would you like me to make you a special home, here in the Mousery? I don't mean a cage, I don't want to shut you up, but somewhere comfy and warm for you? How would you like that?"

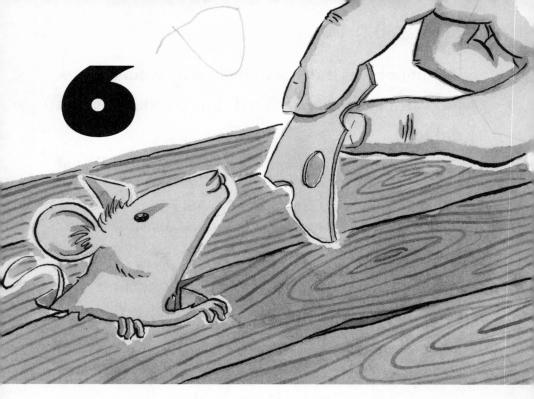

In fact, the Robinson family and their friend Mr. Brown never did get to live in the Mousery at number 16. To be sure, they came up from the cellar whenever they heard the sound of Bill's voice as he talked to his pet mice. They knew he would always give them something to eat.

Beaumont was the first of them who actually took food from the giant's hand, but the others soon did too.

I wanted to tame a wild mouse, thought Bill, *and now it looks as though I've tamed nine! And I daresay there'll be more before long. I must make a proper home for them.*

So one day, when the Robinsons and Mr. Brown came up from the cellar, they found a large shallow box on the floor of the Mousery. Bill had put bedding in it, over which he had scattered a lot of canary seed, and by the time

John Robinson and his family and his old friend had eaten it all, they felt quite at home.

So that when Janet said, "Well, I suppose we'd better get back down to the cellar," John said, "Why?"

"It is very comfortable here, Janet," said Mr. Brown.

"Come on, Mom, let's stay," said Beaumont.

"Yes, let's!" chorused Ambrose and Camilla and Desdemona and Eustace and Felicity.

So they did. But not for long, because soon two things happened. First, the rapidly growing mousekins decided that living with the pet mice was a bit boring, so they went back to the cellar where they could play with their wild friends. Only Beaumont stayed. He liked being with his

friend the giant, and he was interested in getting to know the pet mice. He talked politely to them, and some of them responded in quite a friendly way.

The second thing to happen was that Janet had another lot of babies—nine this time: six boys and three girls.

Gilbert, Hermione, Inigo, Julius, Kingsley, Lindsay, Marmaduke, Niobe, and Olivia.

"Only eleven to go, John," said his old friend, out of Janet's hearing.

"What d'you mean, Mr. Brown?" John asked.

"Eleven more and you'll have finished your first alphabet of names."

"Gosh!" said John, and "Gosh!" echoed Beaumont.

"I only hope," said Mr. Brown, "that I'm still around to see the alphabet completed."

"Why wouldn't you be, Uncle Brown?" asked Beaumont.

"Well, I'm not as young as I was."

"You'll go on for a while yet, Mr. Brown," said John.

But he was wrong.

One morning a few days later, Bill woke up and went into the Mousery to look at what he thought of as his "tame wild mice." There were two boxes on the floor now, for Bill had supplied a small one as a single room for the mouse he thought of as "Granddad."

In the big box Bill could see Janet suckling her newborn nine, watched by John and Beaumont. In the small box Granddad lay comfortably, having breakfast in bed. Not wanting to disturb anyone, Bill tiptoed away.

Mr. Brown spent a lot of his time asleep, but he still had some appetite, and John and Beaumont brought him choice bits of food.

As they had been collecting it that morning, Beaumont said, "You always call Uncle Brown 'Mr. Brown,' don't you, Dad? Why don't you use his first name?"

"I don't know it."

"Can't you ask him?"

"I don't want to. He'd have told me if he'd wanted to."

I'll ask him, thought Beaumont. *I'm sure he wouldn't mind. He's nice, Uncle Brown is. He'll tell me his first name.*

"Uncle Brown," said Beaumont, climbing into the small box that afternoon. "Will you tell me what your first name is? I'd like to know."

The old mouse did not reply.

He has gotten a bit deaf lately, thought Beaumont, and more loudly he said, "Uncle Brown! Can you hear me?"

But there was no answer.

With his nose Beaumont touched the body of the old mouse. It was stone cold.

Just then Bill came into the Mousery with some bits of cookie that he'd saved as a treat for his tame wild mice. He saw that one of the youngsters was in Granddad's box. It looked up at him and squeaked.

"He's dead!" cried Beaumont. "Look, giant, Uncle Brown is dead!"

Oh dear, thought Bill as he stood and stared down. *Poor old Granddad.*

All up and down, in both the even- and the odd-numbered houses in Simple Street, mice were being born. Mice were dying, too, in the jaws of cats or traps, or of poisoning, or simply—like Mr. Brown—of old age. But never before had a mouse been given such a funeral as Mr. Brown was.

"One thing I do know," said Bill Black as he fed his fancy mice, "and that is, I'm not just going to chuck poor old Granddad in the trash. He shall have a proper burial in the garden."

Heaven only knows how Beaumont knew what was going on in the brain of his friend the young giant, but the fact remains that when Bill had dug a hole, he suddenly realized that there were seven little mourners at the graveside. Only Janet could not come out to pay her last respects.

"I can't leave the babies unprotected. Mr. Brown wouldn't have wanted me to," she said to John.

But when Bill had carefully put the body in the grave, John and Ambrose and Beaumont and Camilla and Desdemona and Eustace and Felicity all crept to the edge for a last look at their old friend—"Uncle" to the young ones, "Mister" always to John and Janet, and, had they known it, "Granddad" to the giant who was shoveling the earth back over him.

That night Bill cleaned out the small box on the floor of the Mousery but left it where it was. *It'll do for a spare room*, he thought. *When these nine new mousekins get too boisterous, their parents can get some peace in it.*

Time passed, and at number 16, Gilbert, Hermione, Inigo, Julius, Kingsley, Lindsay, Marmaduke, Niobe, and Olivia went down to join their older brothers and sisters in all the fun

and games that went on in the cellar.
John came out of the spare room
and settled himself comfortably
beside Janet in the big box.

"D'you think we'll have any more
babies, dear?" he asked her.

"I wouldn't be at all surprised," she
replied.

The one member of the family who was
different from the rest—as he always had

been—was Beaumont. Once his father
had left the spare room, he took it
over so he could be near his new friends.

Because he had grown so close to the
young giant, Beaumont had seen a good
deal of the fancy mice. He would go up
and down the cages on the low tables in the
Mousery and chat with them through the bars—
the pink-eyed whites, the black-eyed whites, the

chocolates, the fawns, the plum-colored mice, and the Dutch mice. Most were civil to him (even the bad-tempered pink-eyed buck), and, though he did not know it, quite a few of the young does rather fancied this friendly, talkative young buck.

Bill noticed that his tame pet house mouse spent a lot of time looking and squeaking at one very pretty plum-colored doe. He offered a bit of food to Beaumont, who climbed onto the palm of the giant's hand as usual, and then he popped him into an empty cage and, catching the pretty plum-colored doe, put her in too.

One morning, Bill woke to the sound of much squeaking from the big box on the Mousery floor.

"I want to be alone, John," Janet was saying. "Go away, please."

"Why?"

"I'm going to have some more babies."

"Gosh!" said John.

Don't have more than eleven, he thought, *because then we'll reach the end of the alphabet, like Mr. Brown said. How on earth will I think of names*

*beginning with X or Z? I'll ask Beaumont, he might
know.* But there was no sign of his son.

John climbed up and went along the tables,

looking into each cage. In the last cage of all was a pretty little fancy doe, a plum-colored one, but she was not alone.

"Beaumont!" cried John. "What are you doing in that cage?"

"Just having a chat with a friend, Dad. I'll be out soon. How's Mom?"

"Having babies," said John.

"Gosh!" said Beaumont.

When John returned later to the big box, Janet had had the babies.

"How many?" asked John.

"Eleven," replied Janet.

As they spoke, Bill was letting his pet house mouse out of the fancy plum-colored doe's cage, and soon Beaumont appeared.

"How on earth," his father said to him out of Janet's hearing, "am I going to think of names beginning with X or Z?"

"Easy, Dad," said Beaumont. "Just call it 'Ecks' or 'Zed,' boy or girl. By the way, Dad," he went on, "I think you might like to know something, something that I guess Uncle Brown would have been pleased about."

"What?" asked John.

"Before very long," said Beaumont, "I am going to be a dad, Dad."

"Gosh!" said John Robinson. "My whiskers! Fancy that! And you're right, Beaumont—Uncle Brown would have been very pleased. Gosh!"

GOSH!

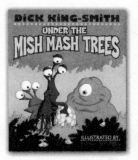

Visit a wonderfully silly nonsense world and the very unusual creatures that live there. You'll meet Wollycobble, Tumblerum, Og, and Ut as they set up house under the mishmash trees.

When a bad-tempered camel escapes from the zoo, he leaves a trail of havoc across the English countryside.

Feathers fly when an intellectual duck decides to take revenge on the farmyard know-it-alls.

When a rampaging tyrannosaurus rex threatens the Great Plain, a pterodactyl and apatosaurus combine their unique skills to take him on in this hilarious adventure.